Farmer
Dray's
farm
Apple Tree
Station
Apple Tree
Village
Church
School
Manor

Farmyard Tales

Woolly Stops the Train

Heather Amery

Adapted by Rob Lloyd Jones

Illustrated by Stephen Cartwright

Reading consultant: Alison Kelly

Find the duck on every double page.

This story is about Apple Tree Farm,

Apple Tree Farm

Poppy,

Sam,

Mrs. Boot,

Ted,

a train

and Woolly.

One morning, Sam, Poppy and Mrs. Boot were collecting eggs.

Ted's tractor rumbled up. Ted looked worried.

"Listen," Ted said.

Toot!
Toot!

It was a train.

“It sounds like it’s in trouble,” said Mrs. Boot.

Toot! Toot!
Toot! Toot!
Let’s go and see.

They rushed to the train tracks.

Toot! Toot!

The train had stopped.

There were sheep on the track!

Oh no!

"It's naughty Woolly," said Mrs. Boot.

She's escaped from her field.

"The other sheep must have followed her."

"We have to move them, but how?"

"Shoo shoo!" said Mrs. Boot.

The sheep didn't move.

"Yaa yaa!" said Ted.
Woolly still didn't move.

"I have an idea,"
said Sam.

"Let's put them on the train!"

Even Woolly liked that idea.

"All aboard!"

Choo
choo!

The train chugged to the station.

The station guard got a surprise.

Goodness me!

It was time to go home.

Sam laughed. “What will Woolly do next?”

Puzzles

Puzzle 1

Put the five pictures in the right order.

A.

B.

C.

D.

E.

Puzzle 2

Find these things in the picture:

tractor	barn	wheels
hens	dog	basket

Puzzle 3

Can you spot the differences between these two pictures? There are five to find.

Puzzle 4

Choose the right sentence for each picture.

A.

"Let's go and see."

"Let's stay here."

B.

There were pigs on the track!

There were sheep on the track!

C.

The sheep ran away.
The sheep didn't move.

D.

"Let's put them on the train!"
"Let's put them on a plane!"

Answers to puzzles

Puzzle 1

1C. 

2E. 

3D. 

4A. 

5B. 

Puzzle 2

barn
dog
wheels
tractor
basket
hens

Puzzle 3

Puzzle 4

A. “Let’s go and see.”

B. There were sheep on the track!

C. The sheep didn’t move.

D. “Let’s put them on the train!”

Designed by Laura Nelson
Series editor: Lesley Sims
Series designer: Russell Punter
Digital manipulation by John Russell

This edition first published in 2016 by Usborne Publishing Ltd., Usborne House, 83-85 Saffron Hill, London EC1N 8RT, England. www.usborne.com

USBORNE FIRST READING
Level Two

USBORNE FIRST READING
Farmyard Tales
Pig Gets Stuck
Illustrated by Stephen Cartwright

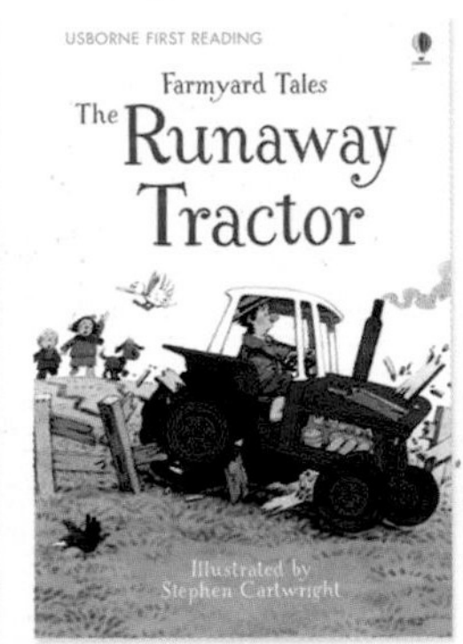
USBORNE FIRST READING
Farmyard Tales
The Runaway Tractor
Illustrated by Stephen Cartwright

USBORNE FIRST READING
Farmyard Tales
The Naughty Sheep
Illustrated by Stephen Cartwright

USBORNE FIRST READING
Farmyard Tales
Tractor in Trouble
Illustrated by Stephen Cartwright

USBORNE FIRST READING
Farmyard Tales
Scarecrow's Secret
Illustrated by Stephen Cartwright

USBORNE FIRST READING
Farmyard Tales
The New Pony
Illustrated by Stephen Cartwright

USBORNE FIRST READING
Farmyard Tales
Pig Gets Lost
Illustrated by Stephen Cartwright

USBORNE FIRST READING
Little Miss Muffet
Retold by Russell Punter
Illustrated by Lorena Alvarez

USBORNE FIRST READING
There Was A Crooked Man
Retold by Russell Punter
Illustrated by David Semple